ROBIN WILLIAMS

A Real-Life Reader Biography

Susan Zannos

Mitchell Lane Publishers, Inc.
P.O. Box 619 • Bear, Delaware 19701

First Printing

Real-Life Reader Biographies

Selena
Tommy Nuñez
Oscar De La Hoya
Cesar Chavez
Vanessa Williams
Brandy
Garth Brooks
Sheila E.
Arnold Schwarzenegger
Steve Jobs
Jennifer Love Hewitt
Melissa Joan Hart
Winona Ryder
Christina Aguilera
Robert Rodriguez
Trent Dimas
Gloria Estefan
Chuck Norris
Celine Dion
Michelle Kwan
Jeff Gordon
Hollywood Hogan
Jennifer Lopez
Sandra Bullock
Keri Russell
Drew Barrymore
Alyssa Milano
Mariah Carey
Cristina Saralegui
Jimmy Smits
Sinbad
Mia Hamm
Rosie O'Donnell
Mark McGwire
Ricky Martin
Kobe Bryant
Julia Roberts
Sarah Michelle Gellar
Alicia Silverstone
Freddie Prinze, Jr.
Rafael Palmeiro
Andres Galarraga
Mary Joe Fernandez
Paula Abdul
Sammy Sosa
Shania Twain
Salma Hayek
Britney Spears
Derek Jeter
Robin Williams
Liv Tyler
Katie Holmes
Enrique Iglesias

Library of Congress Cataloging-in-Publication Data
Zannos, Susan.
Robin Williams / Susan Zannos.
p. cm.—(A real-life reader biography)
Includes index.
Filmography:
ISBN 1-58415-029-7
1. Williams, Robin, 1952 July 21—Juvenile literature. 2. Comedians—United States—Biography—Juvenile literature. [1. Williams, Robin, 1952 July 21- 2. Comedians. 3. Actors and actresses.] I. Title. II. Series.
PN2287.W743 Z36 2000
791.43'028'092—dc21
[B]
00-036533

ABOUT THE AUTHOR: Susan Zannos has taught at all levels, from preschool to college, in Mexico, Greece, Italy, Russia, and Lithuania, as well as in the United States. She has published a mystery *Trust the Liar* (Walker and Co.) and *Human Types: Essence and the Enneagram* was published by Samuel Weiser in 1997. She has written several books for children, including *Paula Abdul* and *Cesar Chavez* (Mitchell Lane).

PHOTO CREDITS: cover: AP Photo; p. 4, 6 AP Photo; p. 9 Corbis/Mitch Gerber; p. 14 Globe Photos; p. 22 Kobal Collection p. 24 Capital/Loftus Corbis; p. 27 Globe Photos; p. 28 Kobal Collection
ACKNOWLEDGMENTS: The following story has been thoroughly researched, and to the best of our knowledge, represents a true story. While every possible effort has been made to ensure accuracy, the publisher will not assume liability for damages caused by inaccuracies in the data, and makes no warranty on the accuracy of the information contained herein.

Table of Contents

Chapter 1
Lonely Boy

In 1997 Robin Williams was named the Funniest Man Alive by *Entertainment Weekly,* a show business magazine. He might be, but that title doesn't fully cover his abilities. It doesn't reveal that he is a serious actor as well as a comedian, or that he's never more serious than when he's being wildly funny.

Robin's comedy routines were the results of his childhood loneliness.

Robin's comedy routines began as the results of his loneliness when he was a child. He was the only child of older parents who each had a grown son from their first marriages. Robin was born on

July 21, 1952, in Chicago. His father was Robert Williams, a successful executive in the auto industry. His mother, who had been a model earlier in her life, was Laurie Williams, a Christian Scientist who believed in self-healing. She was active in charity work. His two half brothers, whom he hardly knew when he was little, are McLauren Smith and Todd Williams. McLauren is a physics teacher in Memphis, Tennessee. Todd is a wine merchant.

Robin Williams is considered one of the funniest men alive.

"My childhood was kind of lonely. Quiet," Robin says. "My father was away, my mother was working, doing benefits. I was basically raised by this maid." Robin spent his childhood on his family's estate in Bloomfield Hills, Michigan, a wealthy suburb of Detroit. He played by himself in the Williams' 40-room mansion.

Robert Williams was a distant man. His son called him Sir and referred to him as "Lord Stokesbury, Viceroy of India." Even as a child Robin turned his painful feelings into comic words. He reports that his earliest efforts at comedy were to make his mother laugh: "My mother . . . was wonderful and charming and witty. But I think comedy was my way of connecting with my mother. I'll make Mommy laugh, and that'll be okay, and that's where it started."

Robin was expected to be self-reliant.

Robin was expected to be self-reliant. He would spend hours playing with his armies of plastic soldiers on a sand table that his father had built for him. He would make up different voices for the soldiers and the officers who led them into battle. At least he did until one day when he was 12. Then his father sat him down and told him about the horrors of his own experiences during World War II. Robert Williams had been on an aircraft carrier when it was hit by a Japanese plane. He had lain bleeding for eight hours. Robin said, "That kind of wised me up." He gave his 2,000 toy soldiers away.

Robin began creating his own characters and voices.

Robin began imitating the routines of television comedians. Jonathan Winters, a comedian who specialized in creating different characters with funny voices, was Robin's favorite. Robin practiced the acts that Winters did. Later he began creating his own characters and voices. All of this was for himself and sometimes for his mother. "It didn't just happen," he said. "It seemed to come naturally once I found it, but I created it through experimentation and playing with different things as a kid."

The Williams family moved to Marin County, north of San Francisco, when Robin was in high school. After high school, he went to Claremont Men's College. He took political science courses, but didn't do well in them. He was much more interested in the improvisation classes that provided him with his first audiences. Improvisation is creating a performance as it happens instead of having a script. Sometimes the classes would perform at mental hospitals in order to find an audience.

Robin's childhood hero was Jonathan Winters, whom he would often imitate.

When he learned that his son wanted to become an actor, Robert Williams suggested that Robin learn welding as an alternate way to make a living, but he did not try to change Robin's mind. Instead his attitude was, "I see you have something you want to do—do it."

Robin wanted to be a serious actor. He decided to leave Claremont College

Robin's classmates would laugh at his comedy routines until they were in pain.

before he graduated. He moved to New York City to attend the famous Juilliard School. John Houseman, a head of the acting school at that time, advised him that classical training was the best approach. Robin was admitted to the third-year program because of his earlier college work at Claremont. But the Juilliard School didn't know how to deal with the wild energy and mad routines of Robin Williams. They asked him to start over as a first-year student.

Although the faculty at Juilliard didn't know what to do with Robin, his classmates would laugh at his comedy routines until they were actually in pain. He did mime, which is acting without sound, on the steps of the Metropolitan Museum of Art to earn money. And he did improvisation at the comedy clubs around New York. Finally, though, the city was too cold and lonely for him. He returned to San Francisco without having graduated from Juilliard, either.

Chapter 2
"That Little Manic Guy"

In San Francisco Robin Williams continued to try out for dramatic roles, but without any luck. He had to work as a bartender to survive. He joined a comedy workshop and began to perform in some of San Francisco's small nightclubs. One of them was a tiny club called the Holy City Zoo, where he started as a bartender and worked his way onto the stage. The comedy club audiences recognized him as "that little manic guy."

Robin had to work as a bartender to survive.

While he was tending bar, Robin met Valerie Velardi, a modern dancer and graduate student who was working as a cocktail waitress. Valerie helped him organize his comedy routines and urged him to try his luck in Los Angeles.

In the summer of 1976, Robin followed Valerie's advice. He appeared at the Comedy Store in L.A. on open mike night, when beginning comedians are given a chance to perform. Robin said later, "My stomach was in my shoes, I was so scared. But after less than a minute I felt comfortable. I knew I could make people laugh."

Robin appeared at the Comedy Store in Los Angeles on open mike night.

Robin soon became a regular performer at the Comedy Store. One night in 1977 he was spotted there by a television producer who was trying to revive the popular comedy television show *Laugh-In.* Robin Williams was hired as the first comedian on the new *Laugh-In,* but the show didn't last long. During that year he also appeared on *The Richard Pryor Show* and on *America 2-Night,* but those shows didn't last long, either.

Robin didn't know it then, but he was about to get his big break. Garry Marshall, the producer of a popular TV series called *Happy Days,* decided to do a show featuring an alien from the planet Ork who lands on Earth. Some famous comedians, including Robin's idol Jonathan Winters, turned down the part. When the producer had open auditions, about fifty actors tried out. Robin was one of them. The director asked if Robin could sit a little differently, the way an alien might. Robin "sat" on his head. They hired him.

When Robin appeared in the *Happy Days* episode in February 1978, the fan mail response was enormous. There was so much mail that Marshall was told to create a spinoff series, which is a new show starring the minor characters from another show. The new show was *Mork and Mindy.* In June 1978, while he was working on the first episodes, Robin married Valerie Velardi.

Mork and Mindy premiered in September 1978 and was an instant hit.

When Robin appeared in *Happy Days,* the fan mail response was enormous.

The television show Mork and Mindy *was an instant hit.*

Mork was a nutty extra-terrestrial who was confused by the way people on Earth do things. Mindy was a twenty-one-year-old girl who helped him understand and kept other people from finding out he was an alien. Mork drank through his finger, talked to eggs and plants, wore his watch on his ankle, and sometimes spoke the Orkian language. He would greet people by saying, "Nanu nanu."

Within two weeks the new show was in the top ten of the Nielsen ratings, which measures the audience for television shows. After that, it was often number one. By early spring of 1979 it was averaging 60 million viewers every week. Children all over the U.S. were imitating Mork and buying Mork dolls and posters.

The critics all agreed that Robin Williams was the reason for the success of the show. Unlike other television shows, which had a written script that the actors learned, *Mork and Mindy* allowed Robin to improvise. The other performers on the show were chosen for their ability to respond to his zany and unpredictable speech and actions. The director of the show said that his job was simply to "make sure Robin doesn't go so far off the wall that only seven people in the audience understand what he's doing."

Unlike other television shows, *Mork and Mindy* allowed Robin to improvise.

Even though Robin had a lot of freedom in playing the part of Mork, he was still afraid that playing only one role would harm his creativity. To avoid this he would go out on weekends and do stand-up comedy routines in Los Angeles nightclubs like the Comedy Store. He told his audiences, "You're only given a little spark of madness. You mustn't lose that madness."

Chapter 3 **Celebrity**

Robin's first LP record sold over a million copies.

The huge success of *Mork and Mindy* made Robin Williams famous. His picture was on magazine covers. In December 1978 he was given the Hollywood Women's Press Club's annual Golden Apple award as the Male Discovery of the Year. He also received a Golden Globe and a People's Choice Award. His first LP album, *Reality . . . What a Concept,* sold over a million copies.

"I found it an incredible high," he said. "Performing is a drug, and you've O.D.'d. It's like bodysurfing on big waves. . . . You get the same rush." He later admitted that he didn't handle his sudden fame well. "It probably happened too fast. It hit me when I was just 25, 26, and I went from zero to 120 mph. No one can teach you or prepare you to deal with it."

Performing wasn't the only high Robin experienced. He began drinking heavily and using cocaine. When asked if his drug use was expensive, he said, "The weird thing about the drug period was that I didn't have to pay for it very often. Most people give you cocaine when you're famous. It gives them a certain control over you; you're at least socially indebted to them."

Robin began drinking heavily and using cocaine.

During this time, Robin and Valerie Williams lived in a house in Topanga Canyon with their dog, a parrot, and some chickens, trying to maintain a casual lifestyle. But it was difficult. Robin's love of performing stand-up comedy in the clubs, and his drinking and using drugs, took more and more of his time. He said later, "Between the drugs and the women and all that stuff, it's all coming at you, and you're swallowed whole."

In 1982, Robin experienced two large shocks that caused him to stop abusing alcohol and using drugs. One was the death of a good friend. Comedian John Belushi died of a drug overdose after Robin had been with him, using cocaine, in his hotel room. The second shock was learning that he was going to be a father. Robin Williams took a serious look at his life and where it was headed. He didn't like what he saw.

Robin took a serious look at his life and where it was headed.

He stopped using cocaine. And he gradually cut down on his drinking, switching from straight whiskey to mixed drinks, and from mixed drinks to an occasional glass of wine. Robin Williams was struggling with the effects of his sudden fame and trying to get his life back on track. He was also trying to get his career on a different track. He still wanted to be an actor as well as a comedian.

His first movie, *Popeye,* was made in 1980. The movie was not a success with either the critics or the public. His next movie was the film version of a popular novel, *The World According to Garp,* in 1982. Again the critics didn't like his acting, feeling that it lacked depth. Robin later admitted that perhaps the problems resulted from his own arrogance and his ambition to be a serious actor. "I was saying, in effect, 'I'll *act.* I'll show you I *can act.*'"

The critics didn't like his acting, feeling that it lacked depth.

Robin made a series of bad movies. He said, "I took on slight projects, thinking, 'I can fix this.' I got suckered into a couple of films like that." Examples of movies that sank like rocks were *The Survivors* in 1983 and *The Best of Times* and *Club Paradise* in 1986.

There was one exception in this string of unsuccessful movies. In 1984, Robin Williams starred in *Moscow on the Hudson.* He played the part of a Russian musician in a circus band. When the circus toured the United States, the musician defected, almost by accident.

Robin kept his sense of humor, and he didn't quit.

The movie shows the difficulties the Russian faces as he tries to survive in the United States. Robin enjoyed making this movie. He said, "Immersing yourself [in] another language and culture is wonderful." Like the alien Mork, the Russian immigrant was an outsider, trying to figure out a strange new world.

In a sense, Robin Williams was doing the same thing in his own life, trying to figure out how to survive in the difficult and confusing world of sudden fame and wealth. He made a lot of mistakes in the process. But like the characters he played, he kept his sense of humor, and he didn't quit.

Chapter 4
Actor

In 1987 Robin Williams finally got the role he had been waiting for. The movie was *Good Morning, Vietnam.* He said that this movie gave him "an opportunity to finally put on screen what I've been doing elsewhere for so long. There have been so many articles about me having this incredible energy on stage but not in the movies. And it's been true."

Robin finally got the role he had been waiting for.

Robin plays the part of Adrian Cronauer, a radio disc jockey working during the war in Vietnam. Cronauer is a favorite of the troops because he plays

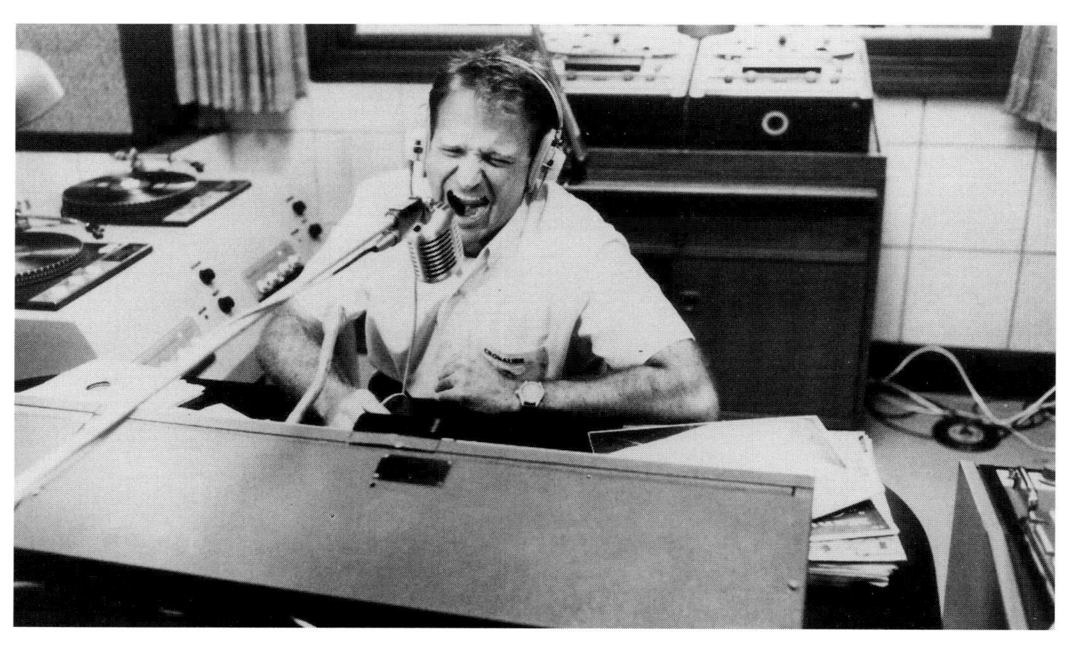

In Good Morning, Vietnam, *Robin played a comic rock 'n' roll disc jockey.*

rock 'n' roll music and uses humor in his broadcasts. In this role, Robin had the chance to do his wild improvisations while he was on the air as a disc jockey. He also demonstrated his serious acting ability as he showed the sensitive young Cronauer experiencing the suffering of the American troops and of the Vietnamese people.

Robin Williams was nominated for an Oscar for his work in *Good Morning, Vietnam.* He received a Golden Globe award for his performance. More important even than the awards was that he was finally considered a serious actor and was offered dramatic roles. In *Dead Poets Society,* he played the part of a teacher at an exclusive boarding school. He inspired his students to love poetry and to follow their dreams. He was again nominated for an Academy Award and a Golden Globe.

By this time Robin was being offered parts he had never dreamed would be available to him. In 1990 he starred in *Awakenings,* playing the part of a doctor who finds a way to help mental patients back to a normal life with special medication. Unfortunately, the effect is only temporary and the doctor is forced to watch his patients return to their hopeless condition. In 1991 Robin starred in *The Fisher King* as a man who suffers a mental breakdown and lives on the streets among the homeless. Again he was nominated for an Oscar for his performance, and he won a second Golden Globe.

Robin was being offered parts he had never dreamed would be available to him.

While Robin Williams' career as an actor was successful beyond his wildest dreams, he was experiencing problems in his personal life. His son Zachary, born in 1983, was the most important thing in Robin's life. But Robin's marriage to Zachary's mother, Valerie, was in trouble. Robin and Valerie separated in 1987 and were divorced in 1988.

Robin with his wife Marsha.

Robin began a relationship with Marsha Garces, the woman who was taking care of Zachary. Newspapers accused Marsha of being a home wrecker even though Robin and Valerie had already separated. This was very painful to both Robin and Marsha, and they tried to protect Zachary from all the bad publicity. They were married in 1989, and their daughter Zelda was born later that year. A son, Cody, was born in 1992.

Robin Williams and his family moved to San Francisco, where they still live. He returned there to get away from the high-pressure lifestyle of Hollywood and to give his family as normal a life as possible. Robin is deeply involved with his children. After he became a father, he appeared frequently in children's movies.

The first of these was *Hook* in 1991. Steven Spielberg's version of the story of Peter Pan stars Robin Williams playing the part of a grownup Peter who has to go back to Neverland to rescue his children from Captain Hook. The following year, Robin created the character of the genie in Disney's *Aladdin.* He was given much of the credit for the success of this animated movie. It was probably the first time improvisation was used to create an animated character. Robin Williams did the improvisations with his voice, and the animators changed the shape of the genie to fit the characters Robin impersonated.

Robin created the character of the genie in Disney's *Aladdin.*

Chapter 5
Keeping the Madness

Robin and Marsha became producers.

Robin Williams was one of the hardest-working actors in Hollywood during the 1990s. He appeared in 27 movies (more than that if his small surprise appearances without screen credits are counted). His movies earned $1.6 billion at the box office. He also had many guest appearances on televison shows such as *L.A. Doctors* and *Friends,* and he continued to do stand-up comedy routines in clubs.

Robin and Marsha Garces became producers. Their first venture was the successful comedy *Mrs. Doubtfire* in

1993. Robin combined his comic genius and his serious acting ability as he played the part of a father whose ex-wife is trying to keep him from seeing his kids. In order to spend time with his children, the father dresses up as a Scottish nanny and gets a job taking care of them. In the process of being a nanny, the father learns how to be more responsible with the kids and more sensitive to his ex-wife.

Mrs. Doubtfire *was the first movie produced by Robin and Marcia.*

Robin is secure in his membership in the $20 million club. This is what they call the small group of actors who make $20 million or more for starring in a movie. It means that audiences will go see a movie just because Robin Williams is in it. The producers and directors know the movie will make money, so they are willing to pay the actor a lot.

The Disney movie *Flubber,* which was a remake of the movie *The Absent-Minded Professor,* was a big hit with kids in 1997. The professor, played by Robin Williams, creates a wildly bouncy substance with many funny uses, but he keeps forgetting to go to his own wedding.

Because of financially successful movies like *Flubber,* Robin has been able to experiment, to accept roles for much lower salaries just because he likes the scripts, and to produce films himself. In the same year, 1997, he appeared as the psychiatrist in the surprise hit *Good Will Hunting.* For this role he received an Academy Award for Best Supporting Actor. It was his fourth nomination, and he finally won.

Robin and Matt Damon worked together in Good Will Hunting, *which won Robin an Academy Award.*

Not all of his movie experiments have been successful financially or critically. In 1999 he produced and starred in a movie called *Jakob the Liar* almost for free.

He said, "I don't care how this will do financially or critically, I'm glad I made it." In the movie, he plays the part of a Jewish man who lies to his neighbors to keep their spirits up during World War II. Neither critics nor audiences liked it. The humor was too dark and the situation too horrible.

Robin Williams experiments with more than just different kinds of movies. He still loves to do live performances. He and his wife are planning a show to take on the road, maybe for as long as six months. "I'll do the whole thing," he says, "from over the Rockies to the wild plains and from clubs to 1,000- or 2,000-seat theaters."

Throughout Robin Williams's career, he has continued to be not only a serious actor and a comedian, but an actor who is serious about comedy. It is the message he brings to his audiences in many of the roles he has played. It is the same message he gave at the beginning of his career in the 1970s: "You're only given a little spark of

Robin has not only been an actor and a comedian, but an actor who is serious about comedy.

madness. You mustn't lose that madness."

In movie after movie, Robin Williams has played characters who refuse to give up their spark of madness, even though they are persecuted by people who are stuffy, cold, and mean. In his first big hit, *Good Morning, Vietnam,* he plays a disc jockey who continues his wild comedy for the troops until he is forced to leave the radio station. In *Dead Poets Society,* he is a teacher who encourages his students to follow their dreams and is fired because of it. In *Patch Adams* he plays a medical student who uses humor to help the patients and is nearly thrown out of medical school by doctors who think they have to be distant and impersonal.

Robin has played characters who refuse to give up their spark of madness.

When Robin Williams speaks to the child and the free spirit in each of us, we realize that nothing is more serious and important than laughter.

Filmography

1980	*Popeye*
1982	*The World According to Garp*
1983	*The Survivors*
1984	*Moscow on the Hudson*
1986	*Seize the Day*
	Club Paradise
	The Best of Times
1987	*Good Morning, Vietnam*
1989	*Dead Poets Society*
1990	*Cadillac Man*
	Awakenings
1991	*The Fisher King*
	Dead Again
	Hook
1992	*Ferngully: The Last Rainforest*
	Aladdin
	Toys
1993	*Mrs. Doubtfire*
	Being Human
1995	*Jumanji*
1996	*Aladdin and the King of Thieves*
	The Birdcage
	Jack
	The Secret Agent
1997	*Father's Day*
	Deconstructing Harry
	Flubber
	Good Will Hunting
1998	*What Dreams May Come*
	Patch Adams
1999	*Jakob the Liar*
	Bicentennial Man
2000	*The Interpreter*
	Don't Worry, He Won't Get Far on Foot

Chronology

- Born July 21, 1952, in Chicago, Illinois
- 1970, attends Claremont Men's College in California
- 1973, attends the Juilliard School in New York City
- Begins performing in comedy clubs in San Francisco in 1976
- Appears as Mork on the TV series *Happy Days,* and stars in the TV show *Mork and Mindy* in 1978
- 1978, marries Valerie Velardi
- 1979, first LP album sells over a million copies
- 1980, begins making movies
- Son Zachary born in 1983
- Is nominated for an Academy Award and wins a Golden Globe for *Good Morning, Vietnam* in 1988
- 1988, divorces Valerie Velardi
- 1989, marries Marsha Garces; daughter Zelda born
- Son Cody is born in 1992
- In 1993, forms production company with wife Marsha
- 1997, named Funniest Man Alive by *Entertainment Weekly*
- In 2000, is listed among the hardest-working actors in show business in the 1990's

Index